ANIMAL RECORD BREAKERS

GOLIATH BEETLE

THE HEAVIEST INSECT

SARAH MACHAJEWSKI

PowerKiDS press

New York

Published in 2020 by The Rosen Publishing Group, Inc.
29 East 21st Street, New York, NY 10010

First Edition

Editor: Theresa Emminizer
Book Design: Reann Nye

Photo Credits: Series Art (frame) HiSunnySky/Shutterstock.com; Series Art (Banners) Roberto Castillo/Shutterstock.com; Series Art (background) Wilqkuku/Shutterstock.com; Cover Yan Lv/Shutterstock.com; p. 5 Nickolas warner/Shutterstock.com; p. 7 https://commons.wikimedia.org/wiki/File:Deinacrida_rugosa_female.jpg; p. 9 DEA / C. BEVILACQUA/ De Agostini/Getty Images; pp. 11, 13 (goliath beetle) 22 Hemera Technologies/ PhotoObjects.net / Getty Images Plus/Getty Images; p. 13 (hercules beetle) Tanawat Palee/Shutterstock.com; p. 13 (titan Beetle) guentermanaus/Shutterstock.com; p. 15 Ines Carrara/ iStock / Getty Images Plus/Getty Images; p. 17 Nick626/Shutterstock.com; p. 19 SHAWSHANK61/ iStock / Getty Images Plus/Getty Images; p. 21 fntproject/Shutterstock.com.

Cataloging-in-Publication Data

Names: Machajewski, Sarah.
Title: Goliath beetle: the heaviest insect / Sarah Machajewski.
Description: New York : PowerKids Press, 2020. | Series: Animal record breakers | Includes glossary and index.
Identifiers: ISBN 9781725308701 (pbk.) | ISBN 9781725308725 (library bound) | ISBN 9781725308718 (6 pack)
Subjects: LCSH: Goliath beetles-Juvenile literature.
Classification: LCC QL596.S3 M325 2020 | DDC 595.76-dc23

Manufactured in the United States of America

CPSIA Compliance Information: Batch #CWPK20. For Further Information contact Rosen Publishing, New York, New York at 1-800-237-9932.

CONTENTS

A REALLY BIG BUG

What is the heaviest bug on Earth? It's the Goliath beetle! Other bugs may have longer or bigger bodies than this beetle, but they don't weigh as much as the Goliath beetle does. When it comes to outweighing the other beetles in the world, the Goliath beetle takes the top prize.

Goliath beetles are really interesting creatures and not just because of their large size. These beastly bugs have an important role in their **ecosystem**. They can also be kept as pets.

Goliath beetles are one of the world's largest insects.

ANIMALS LARGE AND SMALL

Millions of animals call Earth home. The animal kingdom has animals as large as elephants and as small as fleas. Insects are one class, or group, in the animal kingdom. Beetles belong to this class.

Though there are thought to be 350,000 different species, or kinds, of beetles, they have some things in common. Beetles have two pairs of wings. One pair is hard. They have mouthparts specially made for chewing. These are two key characteristics, or features, that make beetles different from other bugs.

ANIMAL ACTION

An insect is an animal that has six legs and one or two pairs of wings.

At 2.5 ounces (71 g), the giant weta pictured here is too heavy to fly. Goliath beetle larvae are even heavier!

THE HEAVIEST INSECT'S HOME

There are many kinds of beetles. So many that scientists believe beetles make up 40 percent—close to half—of all insects. Goliath beetles belong to an insect family called *Scarabaeidae*. There are five species of Goliath beetles. They are some of the largest and heaviest beetles on earth.

Where do Goliath beetles come from? Their habitat, or natural home, is Africa. They live in **tropical** forests that have heavy rains and lots of damp leaves, soil, and wood.

Goliath beetles are built to survive in their habitat.

A BEETLE'S BODY

Like other insects, the Goliath beetle has six legs and two sets of wings. Its body is covered by a hard shell called an exoskeleton. The exoskeleton acts like a suit of armor, **protecting** everything under it.

A Goliath beetle's back is covered with **unique** patterns in black, white, brown, and red. Attached to the back are two sets of wings. One pair is hard and is used for protection. The second pair is soft and is used for flying.

When the Goliath beetle gets ready to fly, watch out! Its wings are almost as long as its body.

The Goliath beetle's hard outer wings protect the soft flying wings, which are folded underneath.

11

BIG AND STRONG

One look at its size shows the Goliath beetle lives up to its name. That, and the fact that this beastly bug can lift 850 times its own weight!

On average, Goliath beetles are between 2 to 4 inches (5 to 10.2 cm) long. But the Goliath beetle is famous because it's so heavy. Adults weigh just under 2 ounces (56.7 g). Compared to the beetle's length, this much weight makes the Goliath beetle the world's heaviest insect.

ANIMAL ACTION

The titan beetle is the longest beetle. Its body is 6 inches (15.2 cm) long. If you measure horns too, the Hercules beetle takes the top prize. It's 7 inches (17.8 cm) long!

MEASURING UP

GOLIATH BEETLE
2 to 4 inches
(5 to 10.2 cm) long

HERCULES BEETLE
7 inches
(17.8 cm) long

TITAN BEETLE
6 inches
(15.2 cm) long

The Goliath beetle has some big buddies.
The titan beetle and Hercules beetle are
longer than any other beetle in the world!

13

THE GOLIATH BEETLE GROWS

The Goliath beetle goes through four stages during its life. These stages make up its **life cycle**. The stages are egg, larva, pupa, and adult. As the Goliath beetle moves through each stage, it goes through a change called complete metamorphosis.

The egg stage is the start of the Goliath beetle's life. Adult beetles lay eggs in dark, wet places, like holes in the dirt or piles of leaves. These conditions keep the eggs hidden from predators. Eggs hatch after two weeks.

ANIMAL ACTION

Butterflies, moths, bees, and mosquitos are other insects that go through complete metamorphosis.

During complete metamorphosis, an insect looks completely different at each stage. A beetle egg looks nothing like the adult it will become!

LARGE, LARGE LARVAE

Most animals are the biggest when they're adults. The Goliath beetle isn't like most animals. Its larvae are almost double the size of adults.

Weighing in at 3.5 ounces (100 g) and measuring up to 5 inches (12.7 cm) long, these huge creatures are bigger than a soda can! Goliath beetle larvae grow big by eating tons of **protein**-rich food. They reach their greatest size after four months. Then it's time for the pupa stage, which the Goliath beetle spends underground.

ANIMAL ACTION

Goliath beetle larvae need more protein than other beetle species. All that protein makes the Goliath beetle larvae famously heavy.

Goliath beetle larvae spend all their time eating.
They're getting ready to become adults.

17

A SEASON OF CHANGES

When the larvae are big enough, they dig **burrows** underground. This usually happens at the end of the rainy season. They'll spend months underground, where amazing changes occur. This is the pupa stage.

During these months, the larvae stop moving and **shed** their skin. They get smaller and start taking the adult form. The wings and exoskeleton form and harden. When the seasons change from dry to wet, Goliath beetles leave their burrows. They are now adult beetles.

Goliath beetle pupae are protected by a hard cocoon, or shell. Heavy rains soak into the ground and soften the cocoon. This is a signal that it's time to come aboveground.

LIFE AS A BEETLE

Male and female Goliath beetles have different characteristics. Their heads are shaped differently. Also, males have Y-shaped horns. They are used when fighting other males for **territory** or for a **mate**.

Adult beetles can fly, and they feed on plant matter. They especially like sweet tree sap. But life as an adult Goliath beetle is all about finding a mate. The new adult females lay eggs, and the life cycle starts over again. This is how the species survives.

ANIMAL ACTION

Goliath beetles like sugary plant food, but they have been known to eat dead plant and animal matter too.

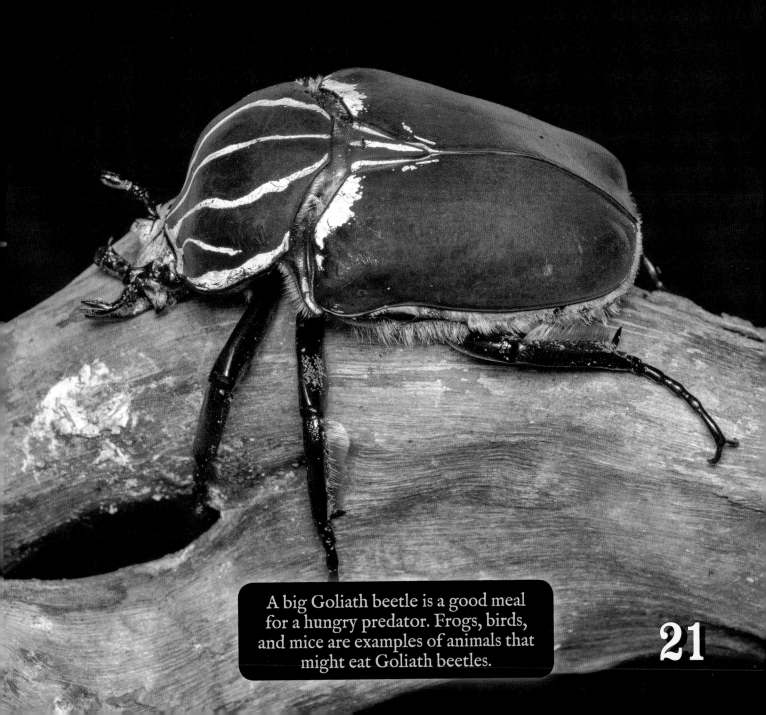

A big Goliath beetle is a good meal for a hungry predator. Frogs, birds, and mice are examples of animals that might eat Goliath beetles.

THE FUTURE OF THE SPECIES

It's no wonder why the Goliath beetle has captured our attention. Not only are these bugs big and heavy, they're surprising in many ways! As larvae, Goliath beetles push the boundaries of nature by weighing as much as a stack of quarters.

Goliath beetles aren't slowing down any time soon. Adults continue to find mates, lay eggs, fly, and feed, just like they're supposed to. This healthy species is here to keep its title as an animal record-breaker. This heavyweight can't be beat!

GLOSSARY

burrow: A hole an animal digs in the ground for shelter.

ecosystem: A natural community of living and nonliving things.

life cycle: All the stages in an organism's life, from birth to death.

mate: One of two animals that come together to produce babies.

protect: To keep safe.

protein: A long chain of structural matter made by the body that helps a cell perform major functions.

shed: To lose or get rid of something.

territory: An area that an animal uses or controls.

tropical: Having to do with an area that is warm and wet.

unique: Special or different from anything else.

INDEX

WEBSITES

Due to the changing nature of Internet links, PowerKids Press has developed an online list of websites related to the subject of this book. This site is updated regularly. Please use this link to access the list: www.powerkidslinks.com/arb/beetle